The Girls FC series

Helena Pielichaty (pronounced Pierre-li-hatty) has written numerous books for children, including *Simone's Letters*, which was nominated for the Carnegie Medal, and the popular After School Club series. A long-standing Huddersfield Town supporter, there are few who could write with as much enthusiasm about girls' football. A local girls' under 11s team helps with the inspiration and tactical know-how, but Helena has been an avid fan of women's football for many years. It clearly runs in the family: her aunt was in a women's team in the 1950s and her daughter has been playing since she was ten (she is now twenty-four!). Helena lives in Nottinghamshire with her husband and has two grown-up children.

Can Ponies Take Penalties?

Helena Pielichaty

WALKER
BOOKS

First published 2009 by Walker Books Ltd
87 Vauxhall Walk, London SE11 5HJ

10 9 8 7 6 5 4 3 2 1

Text © 2009 Helena Pielichaty
Cover illustration © 2009 Sonia Leong

This book has been typeset in Myriad and Handwriter

Printed and bound in Great Britain by Clays Ltd, St Ives plc

British Library Cataloguing in Publication Data:
a catalogue record for this book is available from the British Library

ISBN 978-1-4063-1734-3

www.walker.co.uk

☆ ☆ The Team ☆ ☆

☆ **Megan "Meggo" Fawcett** GOAL

☆ **Petra "Wardy" Ward** DEFENCE

☆ **Lucy "Goose" Skidmore** DEFENCE

☆ **Dylan "Dyl" or "Psycho 1" McNeil** LEFT WING

☆ **Holly "Hols" or "Wonder" Woolcock** DEFENCE

☆ **Veronika "Nika" Kozak** MIDFIELD

☆ **Jenny-Jane "JJ" or "Hoggy" Bayliss** MIDFIELD

☆ **Gemma "Hursty" or "Mod" Hurst** MIDFIELD

☆ **Eve "Akka" Akboh** STRIKER

☆ **Tabinda "Tabby" or "Tabs" Shah** STRIKER/MIDFIELD

☆ **Daisy "Dayz" or "Psycho 2" McNeil** RIGHT WING

☆ **Amy "Minto" or "Lil Posh" Minter** VARIOUS

Official name: Parrs Under 11s, also known as the Parsnips

Ground: Lornton FC, Low Road, Lornton

Capacity: 500

Affiliated to: the Nettie Honeyball Women's League
junior division

Sponsors: Sweet Peas Garden Centre, Mowborough

Club colours: red and white; red shirts with white sleeves,
white shorts, red socks with white trim

Coach: Hannah Preston

Assistant coach: Katie Regan

☆ ☆ Star Player ☆ ☆

☆ **Age:** 9

☆ **Birthday:** 17 April

☆ **School:** Mowborough Primary

☆ **Position in team:** defence

☆ **Likes:** hanging out with friends, especially Megan, and reading

☆ **Dislikes:** horses, ponies – anything that neighs, basically. Oh and Turkey Twizzlers. Yeuw!

☆ **Supports:** England

☆ **Favourite player(s) on team:** Megan

☆ **Best football moment:** lining up for the free kick against the Grove Belles in the summer tournament – that was minty!

Petra "Wardy" Ward

☆ **Match preparation:** I just do stretches and stuff

☆ **Have you got a lucky mascot or a ritual you have to do before or after a match?** No! It's bad enough watching Megan get in a flap over her lucky bandana.

☆ **What do you do in your spare time?** My mum makes me do activities like going to choir and maths club, and playing the clarinet. I could go on, but you'd be sooooo bored!

☆ **Favourite book(s):** The Prisoner's Apprentice by Stephen Elboz, Good Night, Mr Tom by Michelle Magorian, Love That Dog by Sharon Creech and the Lemony Snicket books

☆ **Favourite band(s):** Pink, Dizzee Rascal

☆ **Favourite film(s):** Ratatouille

☆ **Favourite TV programme(s):** Hannah Montana

Hi! My name is Petra Ward and I'm a
Parsnip. That doesn't mean you can
boil me or put me in a soup. It means
I play for the Parrs Under 11s, aka
the Parsnips. My job is to take up the
story where Megan Fawcett, our goalie
and my best friend, left off.

At the beginning of my story we had
only played twice against other teams,
so the summer tournament was meant to
be a fun way of gaining experience.
I'm not sure I found it fun exactly,
but it was certainly an experience!

Read on, amigos,
Petra x

1

It all began like any other Tuesday evening. I got home from school, did my homework (decimal fractions), had dinner (cheese salad and jacket potato). After dinner my sister, Charlotte, and me had an argument about whose turn it was to load the dishwasher (mine), then it was time to go out: me to football training and Charlotte to her riding lesson. So far so normal.

"Don't hang around chatting after practice," Mum called as she dropped me off. "We're picking Dad up at the station afterwards."

"Got you," I said, waving goodbye.

Poor Dad. He's often in London for meetings and not home until late. Poor Mum, too, having to ferry us all around. It wouldn't be so bad if we lived nearer to town, so we could walk or catch buses to places, but we don't. We live in the countryside down a long lane; no buses ever come past. Lornton is the nearest village and that's over a mile away. Luckily for Mum, the Parrs had finished their season so Hannah, our coach, had extended our training time by half an hour, giving Mum more time at the riding school.

I headed straight for the field, where I could see most of the team had gathered. It was a warm evening, so I threw the sweatshirt Mum had made me bring "just in case" on top of the pile with everyone else's "just-in-case" sweatshirts.

Hannah said hello and crossed me off her register, and then I went to find Megan. She was standing near the goalpost with Jenny-Jane Bayliss. "Blimey, Miss Fawcett, what a treat on me peepers it is seein' you 'ere!" I said.

"An' you, Miss Ward," Megan replied, pulling up her socks. "I mean, it must be at least what? An 'ole four hours since we met?"

"Lor! Is it really? Upon my word!"

"What are you two talking like that for?"
Jenny-Jane asked with a frown on her face.

"We're talking Dickens," Megan replied.

The frown deepened. "You can say that again."

"As in *Charles* Dickens. We've been doing the
Victorians, and Miss Parkinson's making us watch
Oliver Twist," I explained.

"The black-and-white version," Megan added
glumly.

"I am dead glad I don't go to your school."
Jenny-Jane sniffed and wandered off.

"Such a sullen child," I told my companion.

Football practice began, as usual, with stretches
and a light jog up and down the training pitch to get
us warmed up. I always enjoy this bit because you
can't really go wrong. It's when we get to the drills I
panic. I'm not exactly what you'd call super-talented
when it comes to football. Ten out of ten for effort,
two out of ten for skill, that's me.

After about five minutes, Hannah told us to put

bibs on and line up. I chose yellow and Megan chose blue. "You look delightful, my dear," I told her. "That shade matches your eyes perfectly."

"And the yellow tones so well with your complexion."

"Thanks a bunch!"

"All right, get into twos," Hannah said. "Blue opposite yellow."

Jenny-Jane, wearing a blue bib, came and stood between us. "Hiya," she said.

I heaved a sigh. This was the third time in a row Jenny-Jane had tried butting in during pairs. "Jenny-Jane, Hannah just said to work in *twos*."

"So?"

"So you can't work with us if that's what you think."

"I could if I wanted." She scowled.

"Yo! One of you over here, pronto!" Hannah called out. "Meggo or JJ. Amy needs a partner."

"I'll give you a thousand pounds and a sausage if you go," Megan told her. "You know how I feel about Amy Minter."

"OK," Jenny-Jane agreed instantly and sprinted off.

"She's *so* annoying," I said as soon as Jenny-Jane was out of earshot.

"She's only doing what she's supposed to be doing. Trying to pair up."

"You don't pair up in threes."

"I know, but she likes being with us; she doesn't know anyone else."

"She doesn't *try* to get to know anyone else!"

Megan looked at me. "Don't be so harsh, Petra."

"Sorry. She's just…"

"Annoying. I know – you said."

"Sorry."

"Stop saying sorry!"

I grinned and pulled my goofy face. "Sorry! Sorry! Sorry!"

"Doofus!" My best friend laughed.

2

"OK, listen up," Hannah began. "We've only got two more training sessions after this one before the summer tournament, so the first thing you all have to learn is to stop running round the pitch like headless chickens."

Dylan McNeil, one of the nutty twins, made a clucking sound and started flapping her arms.

Katie, Hannah's assistant, gave Dylan a gentle nudge. "You should pay attention, Dyl, seeing as you're one of the worst culprits!"

Dylan reacted by putting her hands round her own neck and pretending to strangle herself. She fell to the ground with a final *"Kaw!"* before bouncing up again to listen.

"As I was saying," Hannah continued, "you need to learn that the lot of you running after one ball

while Megan stays in goal is not what we call football
– right?" She stared at us.

We stared back.

"Right?" she prompted.

"Right, coach," we chorused.

"OK. So what we need to look at is passing. Now,
you were pretty good at this in twos and fours last
week, but when it came to the match at the end,
everything went a bit pear-shaped. Any idea why?"
Hannah waited for a moment, then pointed to Lucy
Skidmore. "Lucy?"

Lucy took a deep breath. "In pairs you do softish
passes to your partner so it makes it easy for them,
but on the pitch the ball comes to you any old how
and you haven't time to think. So you just whack it!"

"Give that girl a gold star!" Hannah beamed.
"So this week we're going to look at 'whacking'
it properly so it doesn't go 'any old how'. We call
these whacks volleys, by the way. OK, let's see..."
Hannah looked round and focused on Gemma
Hurst. "Gemma, you were outstanding last week."

"Me?" Gemma said, pointing to herself and going red.

"Yep, you, Miss Natural. Step forward, please."

Gemma stepped into the middle, looking really uncomfortable. I had the feeling she didn't like being the centre of attention.

"When the ball comes to you, instead of bringing it down onto the ground to control it, I want you to let it land on the top of your boot – right on your laces. Like this…" Hannah nodded to Katie, who lobbed the ball so that it landed exactly on top of Hannah's bootstraps.

"Then immediately play your foot forward," Hannah continued. "And direct the ball straight in front of you, keeping your foot raised. That will give it more power, OK?"

Gemma nodded.

"Katie, if you can pass to Gemma this time, please…"

I watched as the ball thudded against Gemma's laces and soared in a perfect arc back towards

Katie. Katie brought it down in front of her and gave Gemma a thumbs-up. Hannah made Gemma repeat the volley a few more times. She made it look so easy!

Then it was our turn.

As usual, Megan was miles better than me. "I'm rubbish," I said as I mis-kicked another of her passes and ended up spinning right round.

"You're not," Megan said. "You just *think* you are, so you fluff it."

"Humph!" I said and tried again.

"Toe-poke!"

"Toe-broke, more like!" I sighed. I'd never get the hang of this stuff.

We spent another hour on different drills, then finished with a short six-a-side match.

It didn't seem like a whole hour and a half had gone by when Hannah said, "OK, girls, that's it. Same time next week. Don't forget to take a letter home about the final details of the tournament."

"Does it *have* to be at Ashtonby?" Megan asked,

scowling at her sheet when she got it.

"Yes, why?"

"'Cos the blooming Grove Belles are good enough already without them having home advantage."

"They've also got facilities advantage." Hannah laughed.

"Huh! They would have!"

As we trundled off the pitch, Megan linked her arm through mine. "So, me old covey, how brilliant was that out of ten?"

Truth? Five or six. "Eight point seven," I said instead.

"I give it twenty!"

I rolled my eyes and laughed. "You would!"

3

Mum was waiting in the car park, the car engine revving. "Come on, Petra. Dad's train gets here in ten minutes."

"All right, keep your wig on, missus," I said.

I clambered into the back of the Range Rover and sat next to Charlotte. I can tell you everything you need to know about my sister in two words: Pony Mad. She's totally bonkers about the things. If she could, she'd be superglued to Betty Boo's saddle and stay on her for ever, like a centaur.

"Yeuw! You smell of disgusting horses!" I said, wrinkling my nose.

"You smell of disgusting football," she said, pushing me away.

I pushed her back and we had this play fight until Mum told us off for distracting the driver.

Once we got onto the main road, Mum told Charlotte to tell me the fantastic news.

"Oh, Mum, it's not *that* fantastic," Charlotte mumbled.

"It is so!"

"It's not!" Charlotte insisted. She rolled her eyes at me as if to say sorry. She reminded me of Gemma Hurst not wanting any limelight but being forced into it anyway. It couldn't stop Charlotte keeping the excitement out of her voice, though. "I've been chosen to be in the Pony Club junior show-jumping team at Applehampton!"

"Go you! Well done, sis."

"Thanks."

"You see, these are things *you* could be getting involved in if you joined the Pony Club, Petra," Mum said.

"Mum, I do loads of stuff I hate already!"

"Such as?"

"Clarinet, maths club, choir…"

"Don't exaggerate! You don't *hate* any of them."

"Wanna bet?"

"Wanna?" Mum pounced. "Wanna?"

"*Want to.*"

"Thank you. Anyway, I'm talking outdoor things, Petra. Sport."

"I play football!"

"I mean a *suitable* sport."

"Football *is* suitable."

"What? Running around a field chasing a ball? It can't possibly compare to the thrill of jumping over hedges!"

"It can."

"How?"

"Well … can ponies take penalties?"

There was a short pause before Charlotte started snorting with laughter. "She's got you there, Mum!"

Mum gave one of her deep, disappointed sighs. "I just think it's a shame, that's all, Petra. You miss out on so much!"

I fumbled in my kit bag for the letter from Hannah. "No I don't. Look! I'm in a tournament too! Saturday the tenth at Ashtonby Sports Ground."

"The tenth? That's when mine is!" Charlotte grinned – then bit her lip as she realized at exactly the same time as me what that meant. Problems! Ashtonby and Applehampton are about forty miles apart.

"Oh, typical!" Mum said as we pulled into the station. "Another weekend when I'm meant to be in ten places at once."

"I told you about my tournament *weeks* ago," I reminded her. "You wrote it on the calendar." The Pony Club calendar, of course.

"Hmm! Well, that doesn't solve the problem."

"It's OK, you don't have to come," I said. "Dad can take me."

No such luck. "Sorry, sweetheart." He sighed when I showed him the form during supper. "I'm not home that weekend."

"Oh?" said Mum. Dad often worked away from home mid-week, but not usually at weekends.

"It's the final presentation on the tenth, remember? We've got people coming from all over Europe. I have to be there." He handed the letter back to me and patted my head. "Next time, eh?"

"Do you *have* to be at the tournament, Petra?" Mum asked.

"Yes."

"But is it crucial that you're there? Will the team have to pull out if you don't turn up?"

This was a trick question, I could tell. "Noooo," I admitted. "It's seven-a-side and there's twelve of us, but..."

Mum leaned across and patted my head just like Dad had. "Well then, you can sit this one out. I have to put Charlotte first on this occasion; this is a really big chance for her."

"Mum!"

But that was it as far as Mum was concerned. End of. "Right, let's get that dishwasher loaded. Whose turn is it?"

4

At breakfast the next morning, Charlotte was extra nice to me. "Did you sleep OK?" she began.

"So-so," I mumbled.

"Do you want any toast? Or cereal? Cup of tea? Orange juice?"

I just shrugged.

She poured a glass of orange and set it in front of me. "What lessons have you got at school?"

Another shrug.

"Or is it DVDs and games, with it being the last day before we break up?"

Guess what? I just shrugged again.

"Though knowing Miss Parkinson she'll make you carry on as usual. I remember when I was in her class we had to sit through *Oliver Twist* on the last day when everyone else was watching *The Emperor's New Groove*."

I was just about to shrug again – but Charlotte was trying so hard I thought I'd put her out of her misery. "Got it in one."

"No way! Really?"

"Charlotte, listen, you don't have to suck up to me; I know it's not your fault you're the favourite. I don't hate you or anything."

She sighed and plonked a huge plate of thickly sliced buttered toast and a jar of blueberry jam under my nose. "Mum just loves horses," she said. "It's her blind spot."

"I know."

"I suppose it's my blind spot, too," she admitted, pulling her ponytail out of her cereal bowl. (See, even her hairstyle is named after those creatures!) "But I've been thinking ... what if I go to Applehampton with Sophie? She's on the team, too. Then Mum could take you to the football."

I felt my hopes rise. "Would Mum agree to that?"

"She might," Charlotte replied, but I could tell she was not a hundred per cent confident. Or even *one* per cent.

I felt my hopes drop right back to where they belonged. "She won't. You know she won't. Not if it's between show jumping and football. No way."

Charlotte chewed her bottom lip. That meant she knew I was right.

"Nice try, though," I said.

"How's everyone else getting to Ashtonby?"

"Cars, I suppose."

"Well, why don't you ask Megan if you can travel with her?"

You know that sound the microwave makes when it's finished zapping a ready meal to death? That "ping" sound? That's what my brain did then. Ping! I'll repeat that so you get the full effect. *Ping!* "That's a brilliant idea, Charlotte!" I said and reached for the toast and jam. "I don't know why I didn't think of it."

5

At school, I cornered Megan while she was on pencil-sharpening punishment.

Miss Parkinson gives rubbish jobs like that to people all the time. I can't remember what Megan did to deserve the pencil punishment. She probably breathed out at the wrong time or something.

I get the feeling Miss P. would love to have been a teacher in Victorian times, swishing her cane around and tugging her pupils' ears. I am so glad I only have one more day in her class.

"Course we'll pick you up," Megan said when I told her about my problem. She finished sharpening the final pencil, then blew the shavings into the bin. "Hey, why don't you come on Friday night and sleep over?"

"Oh, bless yer dear heart!" (Can you tell we'd

just watched the end of *Oliver Twist*?)

"It'll be wicked." Megan grinned. (Guess who'd doodled all the way through?)

"Truly, it shall."

"And Jenny-Jane will be staying too."

Talking Dickens went straight out of the window then. There was a long pause before I replied. "Er … will she?"

"Yes. I asked her last night after training."

"Oh." Trust Jenny-Jane to muscle in the second I'd gone. The longer training sessions meant I didn't go back to Megan's Auntie Mandy's to wait for Mum any more. Obviously *someone* did, though.

"She was telling me about her horrible—"

"Horrible what?" I interrupted. "Tackles?"

Megan looked up and shrugged. "Nothing. Never mind. Hey, if you come too it means we can play three-and-in down the park!"

"Yeah!" I said, putting as much enthusiasm into my voice as I could.

"Cool! And you can help me with my goalkeeping. Katie said I need to…"

"If you two have finished your little chat, I'd like to take the register," Miss Parkinson called across.

Megan turned to her. "It's not a little chat, Miss; it's about football. That makes it a big chat. Of national importance, probably."

It's a good job it was our last day in Miss Parkinson's class because I had the feeling Megan would have been sharpening pencils for ever otherwise.

6

So the summer holidays began. The minty bits of that are no school and longer in bed of a morning but the not-as-minty bits are not seeing friends and especially not seeing Megan. Living in the countryside is great for fresh air and all that nature stuff, but it sucks for hanging out with friends. When I hear people at school saying they'll call round for each other I'm really envious. Calling round for my mates involves at least twenty thousand texts and five phone calls!

Still, at least I had the tournament to look forward to – especially as Megan's mum had said no problem to me being at Megan's the night before for the sleepover. Then there was training on top. Yes! Bring it on!

By the time the following Tuesday arrived, I was

so excited about going to football practice I was practically bundling Mum into the car. "Come on! Giddy up!" I told her, thrusting the car keys into her hands. I find she responds better if I use horsey terms.

"Well, I really don't know where this love of silly football comes from," she protested. "Now rugby I could understand … or cricket … but *football*…"

I didn't tell her it wasn't silly football I loved but the silly people playing silly football.

7

As soon as Mum pulled up in Lornton FC's car park, I unclipped my seatbelt and shouted "Smell you later!" before dashing towards the field. "Hello, Parsnips!" I yelled, throwing my "just-in-case" top down on the other "just-in-case" tops and water bottles again.

Megan, doing keepy-uppies, looked up and grinned. "Thirteen ... fourteen ... I'm glad you're here! Loads of people are missing. Fifteen ... sixteen..."

I looked round and realized she was right. Holly was standing next to Nika, and next to Holly was Tabinda. Lucy and Gemma were chatting together by the goalposts – but that was it. There were only seven of us. Even Jenny-Jane was missing, and she *always* comes. I tried not to feel glad but I couldn't help it; at least I could pair up with Megan in peace.

"Oh well … I'll just have to run twice as fast!" I said.

Megan laughed and called a halt to her keepy-uppies. "Yeah! Me, too!" She tucked the ball under her arm and walked with me towards Hannah.

We stood in a small circle while Hannah took the register. "Right then. I know Eve and Amy are on holiday, but does anyone know anything about the twins?"

"They're just arriving," Holly said. "Late as usual."

We all turned to see the McNeils' orange camper van swing into the car park. The middle door was drawn back and first Daisy, then Dylan jumped out, whooping and yelling. "Wait for us! Wait for us!" They sprinted towards the field, but turned when someone called from the van and a bag was tossed onto the ground. "Och! Hoots mon! Ma boots mon!" Daisy cried and went back for them.

"What about JJ?" Hannah continued.

"Do you want me to go and see? She only lives over there," Megan said. She pointed to the row of houses that backed onto the playing field. I knew the one with the England flag hanging in one of the bedroom windows was Jenny-Jane's.

"No," Hannah said, "we'd better crack on."

"I don't mind going to check."

"No worries. I'm sure she'll come if she can," Hannah said and clapped her hands. "OK, girls, let's warm up. In a line, please..."

"I wonder where she is?" Megan asked me as we all spaced out along the touchline.

"No idea."

We began to jog, and all reached the halfway line in a perfect row.

"Excellent," Hannah complimented. "Keep together. Always be aware of one another's pace and positioning..."

"She said she was coming when I saw her yesterday," Megan mumbled.

"Sorry?"

Megan glanced towards the houses again.

"When I called round for Jenny-Jane yesterday.

She said she was coming."

I felt a small lump in my throat. "How come you called round for her yesterday?" I asked. I'd been really bored yesterday. I'd even practised the clarinet without being forced into it by Mum.

"And turn!" Hannah instructed.

"We were watching the Parrs doing extra training."

"Oh. I thought they'd stopped – I thought that's why we had longer..."

"They had, but they're touring Ireland for a week in August, playing other women's teams pre-season, so they have to get up to match fitness."

"Oh," I said as Megan twisted away from me and I twisted away from her. "I didn't know that."

"And again!" Hannah repeated.

"I always watch them if I can," Megan said as we faced each other again.

"Oh."

"You know I do."

"Well, I didn't know Jenny-Jane did, too."

"Does it make a difference?" Megan asked.

"No, of course not!" I replied. I admit I may have sounded a bit shirty when I said that.

Megan picked up on it straight away. "Huh!"

"Huh what?"

"You're doing it again!"

"Doing what?"

"Being funny about JJ."

"Now bend and touch the ground!" Hannah said.

"Funny?" I said as Megan's head disappeared. I bobbed down a beat later. That meant we were out of sync the rest of the way.

Me (to Megan's trainers): "I'm not ..." – bob – "... funny ..." – bob – "... about her."

Megan (to top of my head): "OK ..." – bob – "... if you ..." – bob – "... say so."

Me (to trainers): "I think ..." – bob – "... she's OK ... It's just..."

Megan (to my nose): "Just what?"

Me (to Megan's knees): "Nothing."

Megan (to my nose again): "Nothing much! You are such a fibber."

I opened my mouth in surprise, then closed it
again. Megan had never called me a fibber before.
Not in a serious voice like she meant it. Never ever!

I couldn't dwell on it, though, because Hannah
brought us together to tell us about the first drill.

We had to grab a ball each and line up behind
the cones. I lined up between Megan and Holly and
looked at my feet, one foot steadying the ball as
instructed.

"Five quick toe-taps!"

We did five quick toe-taps.

"Now I want to see you all dribbling between the
cones. Off you go," Hannah directed.

I did my best – this was basic – but Hannah still
told me I needed to keep the ball closer to my feet.
"If you kick it too far ahead it makes it too easy for
the opposition to nip the ball away," she said.

I turned to Megan on my right and sighed.
"Maybe *I* should stay and watch the Parrs train
in future. I might learn something!"

She dribbled back to the touchline, stopped and

then grinned at me. "Oh, Petra, do me a favour!"

"Do you a favour?"

"Don't be such a fake!" she said. "It's obvious you only want to come and watch the Parrs because I said JJ did."

"I never!"

"Keep moving, you guys! No time for gossip!" Hannah called across.

Megan set off upfield again, head down, eye on the ball, dribbling between the cones with ease. I just stood there, staring after her. First I was a fibber and now I was a fake.

In the short match at the end I made a mess of every ball that came near me. I either whacked it into orbit or passed it to someone on the opposite side or missed it altogether. "Come on, Petrasaurus, wake up!" Daisy told me as I sent her a clod of grass instead of the ball.

It will come as no surprise if I tell you I did not give training even a five or a six out of ten this time. More a three-point-one.

8

I spent a couple of days in a bad mood, thinking about Megan calling me a fibber and a fake, but by the end of the week I was over it. In fact, if that policeman hadn't come to the house when he did, I'd have turned up at training the Tuesday after and everything would have been minty. *If* that policeman hadn't come.

I was in the middle of tidying my bedroom when he arrived. I was arranging my books in alphabetical order on the windowsill, and was just deciding whether Cliff McNish should go before or after Colin McNaughton when I glanced out of the window and saw a police car pull up outside our main gate. A police officer with grey hair and a craggy face got out of the car and began walking towards the front door.

The last time a policeman had come to our house it was for a house-to-house inquiry about a murder in Saddlebridge. It had been the first murder there in over a hundred years – that's almost back to Victorian times. Maybe there'd been another one? I ran downstairs as fast as I could and almost broke my neck on the flex from the Hoover. "Mum, Mum, it's the police!" I gasped dramatically just as the doorbell rang.

Mum switched the vacuum cleaner off and told me to calm down. "It'll just be Derek," she said. "Go and let him in."

It turned out she was right. It was "just" Derek. I don't know why I was surprised Mum knew the police officer by his first name; she's lived round here all her life so she knows everybody. Mum made Derek a cup of tea while I fetched the biscuit tin. I hovered around, but she did this thing with her eyebrows, which she does when I'm in the way so I knew I'd better scram.

I found out straight after he'd gone why he'd

visited, though. "Right," Mum announced, rummaging in the key box we kept behind the fridge freezer. "Action stations."

"Why?"

"Derek's just told me the Bayliss brothers are back. That means I'd better start locking up all the sheds and outhouses again."

"Why? Who are they?"

"Who are they? Brendan and Billy Bayliss, Lornton's own mini crime-wave, that's who. Burglaries and break-ins have plummeted since they went to jail, but they've been let out three months early. Typical!" She strode outside towards the first shed, where she kept all her gardening tools and equipment.

"Did you say Bayliss?" I asked.

"I did. They live opposite the football ground in Lornton."

It had to be Jenny-Jane's family. See, I knew there was something fishy about her!

"Villains through and through, the lot of them.

Their dad was a bad 'un. And their grandad. It runs in the family," Mum fumed. She yanked open the shed door and began searching in the wheelbarrow for the discarded padlocks. "Every Bayliss who's ever lived in Lornton has had a police record, man and boy."

"Really?"

"Their mother must be very proud!"

I frowned at first, wondering why she would be – then realized mum was being sarcastic. "Oh."

I followed her round while she locked and bolted every hut, outhouse, barn and shed. At the stables, she warned Charlotte to make sure any valuable tack was out of sight. It scared me a little, seeing how serious Mum was taking PC Just-Derek's news.

9

Of course, I telephoned Megan to tell her what had happened. "... and Mum says they're villains through and through," I finished, pacing up and down our entrance hall, "so please be careful if you visit Jenny-Jane's house, won't you? And hide your purse."

There was a pause at the end of the line. "That's so judgemental, Petra."

"Why?"

"Jenny-Jane isn't like her brothers!" she replied. Her voice was really cold.

"I'm not saying she is," I began, though if I'm honest I suppose I had been. "I'm just telling you in case you didn't know and they pinched something ... or something..."

"Of course I knew! I tried telling you about her

brothers once, but you wouldn't listen."

I stopped pacing and frowned. When had she done that? I didn't remember.

Not that Megan gave me a chance to remember. "And yes, they are as bad as your mum says," she conceded, "but it's nothing to do with JJ."

"I guess."

Personally, I wasn't so sure. I had this picture of the Bayliss family all sitting together in the kitchen, a mountain of stolen goods on their table, with Billy (I imagined him to be like Fagin in *Oliver Twist*) saying to Jenny-Jane, "Have whatever you want, our kid. That MP3 player's a beaut. Got it off this woman down town..."

Megan soon put me right. "For your information, they're horrible to Jenny-Jane; they bully her all the time."

That took me by surprise. "Do they?"

"Yes, they do. She was really gutted when she found out they'd been let out early."

"Oh," was all I could think of to say. I now had this

picture of Jenny-Jane being offered the MP3 player and shaking her head. "No way!" she snarled at Billy, who in my head I had swapped from Fagin to the even creepier Bill Sykes.

Megan's voice was still icy cold. "Do you know why she wasn't at training on Tuesday?"

"No."

"They wouldn't let her out because she answered them back. They blocked the door every time she tried to escape."

"Oh." I went from disliking Jenny-Jane to feeling really sorry for her in an instant. Her life sounded miserable.

"Would you want to live with people like that?" Megan asked, her voice rising higher and higher. It does that when she gets worked up about things. I knew I'd really upset her with what I'd said about Jenny-Jane, but I hadn't meant to. I had only wanted to warn her.

"No, of course not, I'd hate—" I began, but she didn't let me finish my sentence.

"Me neither; that's why I've invited her to stay at my house. She needs to be calm before the tournament."

"Course. I'll be extra—" I would have said "nice", if I'd been given the chance.

"I've got to go," Megan interrupted again. "I'll call you later."

OK, I thought, staring at the phone. I shook my head and turned, about to finish off tidying my bedroom, when the phone rang again. "Five Gate Farm," I said.

"Petra? It's me, Megan," Megan said – as if I wouldn't know her voice anywhere.

"Wow! Is it 'later' already?"

"I've been thinking … I think it's best if I cancel the sleepover."

Megan said it so quickly I wasn't sure I'd heard right. "Really?"

"Really. You know how stressed I get before a match, and I think if you and JJ are together it would just make me worse."

I felt my stomach clench. She was cross with me
– and I didn't blame her! "No it wouldn't. Now that
you've told me about her brothers, I understand
more. I'll make an effort."

Megan sighed. "You say that now, but I'd just be
on edge all the time, in case. Let's just leave it."

"But…"

"Let's just leave it, please?"

"OK," I agreed, "if that's what you want."

"It is."

"There'll be other sleepovers," I said, trying to
sound perky, even though I'd been really looking
forward to staying at her house, especially as I knew
Mum and Charlotte would be so uptight the night
before Applehampton. Jenny-Jane wasn't the only
one who could do with a calm atmosphere.

"My dad'll still pick you up," Megan continued.
"Eight o'clock OK?" She sounded more like her old
self now, thank goodness.

I breathed a sigh of relief. "Brill. And look, Megan,
when your dad picks Jenny-Jane up, let me sit in

the back with her. I'll make a proper effort this time. I promise I'll not say a thing about her brothers or anything."

There was a short gap before she spoke again. "Jenny-Jane's still coming to stay, so she'll already be in the car," Megan said quietly.

My stomach buckled as if a slab of uncooked pastry had been dropped into it. "She's staying over but I'm not?" I asked.

"She needs to be calm before the tournament…" Megan repeated.

"And I don't?"

"Well, obviously you need to be calm too, but you *will* be calm because you're always calm. You're a calm person … and you live in a calm house."

Calm house? I thought about Mum frantically locking everywhere up earlier on. That wasn't what I'd call calm. Nor was how I was feeling right now. And what Megan said next didn't help.

"And, let's face it, you only wanted to come because it's a sleepover, not because it's football."

"'Scuse me?"

"The football bit's not that important to you."

"What do you mean?"

"Well, you *do* only play because I do. You'd never have thought of going to football otherwise. That's the main difference between you and JJ, you see."

"What is?"

"Well, that JJ would turn up to football whether I was there or not; she'd go whatever."

"Because I'm a fake, like you told me last time, and she's not?" I said. My voice came out in a whisper.

I think Megan realized she'd gone too far then. "Oh no, that's not what I'm saying…" she began, but it was too late. I knew exactly what she was saying. I got the message loud and clear. What she was saying was that I, Petra Ward, only turn up to practice every week because I'm so pathetic I have to copy everything she does. Well not any more, sunshine.

I took a deep breath and cleared my throat. My hands were shaking as I clasped the phone.

"OK, well … er … I guess in that case I won't turn up at all then."

"Oh, come, come, Miss Fawcett, don't go fretting your eyelids!"

Huh! If Megan thought she could get round me by using silly Dickens talk she had another think coming! "Get lost!" I told my ex-best friend. "Get totally lost."

Then I hung up and burst into tears.

It took me ages to stop crying, but after about half an hour I managed to just get down to sniffling and nose-blowing level. When Mum saw me she asked what was wrong, and I told her I thought I had a cold coming and I wanted to go to bed early. "That's a good idea," she said. "You don't want to pass it onto Charlotte."

I headed upstairs. I didn't even wait up for Dad's nightly phone call or brush my teeth. I just slid into bed, pulled the duvet right over me and closed my eyes.

10

The next morning the heavy-pastry feeling was worse than ever. I plodded downstairs to the kitchen, still in my PJs, where Mum cornered me as I was helping myself to a cream cracker.

"Ah, so you're up!" she said. "How are you feeling?"

"Not great," I said, which was true.

She strode towards me and laid a hand on my forehead. "Mmm. Your head's quite hot and you do look peaky. Why don't you go back to bed for the morning?"

"I might…"

She did her hairy-eyebrow thing. "Not *might*, young lady. Definitely. You don't want to spread cold germs around. Summer colds are as nasty as winter colds, and if Charlotte comes down with something this week her performance will be affected..."

Charlotte, Charlotte, Charlotte! If I didn't like my sister so much I'd probably have to put slug pellets in her cornflakes or something.

"I'll bring you up some honey and lemon as soon as I've fed the hens."

"All right," I said, and sloped off back to my bedroom.

Up there, I discovered that falling out with friends and having a cold have got very similar symptoms:

☆ You feel funny

☆ You can't concentrate

☆ Your eyes sting with tears

☆ You blow your nose a lot

The main difference is that when you have a cold and friends phone or text you to see if you are OK you can usually sniffle a few words to them, but when Megan called just after lunch I wouldn't talk to her. Not the first time, nor the second, nor the third. I was tempted to sometimes, but then I'd remember what she'd said and why I'd fallen out with her in the first place, and I'd end up feeling angry all over again and shaking my head when Mum or Charlotte told me who was on the line or just deleting her message when she texted.

In the end she took the hint and stopped calling.

Another thing I discovered was that even though pretending to have a cold and staring into space can make an hour seem like ten hours, time still passes. Before I knew it, it was time for football training again. Not just any old football training, but the last training session before the tournament. The one where they gave out all the details of the matches we'd be playing and where to go and what to do. Pity I wouldn't be there. "I think I'll give training a miss," I told my mum. "I'm still not over my summer cold." I couldn't bring myself to tell her what had happened just yet. I couldn't stand the cross-examination.

Mum didn't mind at all. "That's very sensible of you, Petra. You can come and watch Charlotte instead. It means we don't have to leave early to pick you up and she can have longer on the jumps."

"Great," I mumbled.

So I stood watching Charlotte and her team jump over fences and bales of hay for two hours, trying my best not to think about what Megan and the others would be doing.

Don't even go there, I told myself sternly. Your time in the team is like your friendship with Megan. *Finito*. No more. So over. "Mum," I said, shaking her arm to get her attention.

She glanced round at me and smiled. "Did you see Charlotte? A clear round!"

"Yes," I fibbed.

"The team coach will put her on fourth on

Saturday if she has any sense. Betty Boo's a calm horse; that's what you want from your last rider – someone calm and steady."

Calm! Did she have to use that word? "Mum, if you wouldn't mind giving me your attention for one tiny second," I said, my eyes welling with tears.

She looked concerned and put her hand on my forehead again. "Oh dear, aren't you feeling well again? Do you want to go and sit in the car?"

"No! I just want to tell you I'm not going to the tournament on Saturday."

Her whole face lit up. "Really?"

"Yes. I'm not … I'm not bothered about football any more."

"Ha! I knew it was just a phase."

"Yes," I said. "You were right."

The strange thing was I thought the heavy-pastry feeling would disappear when I told her that, but it didn't. It just turned into cement instead.

11

Next morning Mum sent me down to the stables with a long list of things for Charlotte to do. "She left it on the kitchen table, silly girl. You can tell the stress is getting to her, poor thing. Take her a snack – and some water, too."

I arrived at the stables just as Charlotte was leading Mum's horse, Ginger, into the paddock. "Oh no, what now?" Charlotte asked when she saw me.

"Nice welcome!"

"She's sent you with the list, hasn't she?"

"She might have," I said.

Charlotte patted Ginger on the rump and closed the gate behind him. "She's driving me nuts! I've done everything on that list twice. If she gives me one more piece of advice about Saturday I'm going to scream." She strode towards the stables again.

"I've brought you a KitKat too," I called after her.

"Hang on, I just need to check the haynets and fetch Betty Boo."

She disappeared into the stables for a few minutes. I didn't follow her. The stables make me feel claustrophobic, especially if the other horses are there too, following you with their huge heads and liquid black eyes. Eugh!

A few minutes later she came out again, leading Betty Boo by a leather rein. Betty Boo is a Welsh grey mare – but don't ask me how old she is or how many hands high and stuff like that. She's way bigger than me and whinnies a lot; that's all you need to know. I stood well back as Charlotte tethered Betty Boo to the fence.

"How's your bogus cold?" she suddenly asked me, patting Betty Boo's mane.

I frowned. "'Scuse me?"

"Your bogus cold. How is it? And when are you going to fess up to what's *really* going on?"

"I ... I don't know what you mean."

"Tch! Yeah, right," Charlotte scoffed before disappearing into the stables again.

This time she came back carrying a lilac and black rucksack over her shoulder. She threw it down near Betty Boo, pulled an old towel from the side pocket, spread it out on the ground and started whipping out all sorts of combs and brushes and bits of kit for grooming. It looked like a giant's manicure set.

Charlotte grabbed a curry comb and began brushing Betty Boo's coat. "So," she said, "tell me."

"Tell you what?"

"Why you've dropped football. I don't believe for one second you've lost interest, just like that. Come on, spill."

I focused on the long metal hoof pick in the manicure set, but it kept going blurry. "OK." I sniffed. "The thing is, I've kind of fallen out with Megan."

"Well, dur! I know that! What I *don't* know is how come?"

I suppose I shouldn't have been surprised she'd

noticed. Charlotte is pretty observant. She's good at choosing times to talk, too. Like now. I took a deep breath and, as Charlotte brushed Betty Boo's coat, I blurted out everything.

"That doesn't sound like Megan," Charlotte said matter-of-factly.

"Well, it's what happened."

Charlotte paused mid-stroke. "It's her blind spot," she said.

"What is?"

"Football. Football's Megan's blind spot, just like horses are mine and Mum's."

"I suppose."

"And Megan's yours."

"Megan's my blind spot?"

Charlotte looked up at me and nodded, then began brushing Betty Boo again. "Megan's your blind spot. You've always been a bit clingy with her."

"Well, I'm not now!" I bridled. "I'm as cling-*less* as you can be."

"OK – don't get all radgy with me; I'm just saying."

I stood there fuming for a few seconds while Charlotte swapped curry combs and started on Betty Boo's mane.

"So where does that leave football?" Charlotte asked.

"What do you mean?"

"Well, if you're so quick to pack it in, that means Megan's right. You *do* only go because of her."

"Thanks for taking her side!" I said, my eyes starting to fill with tears.

"I'm not taking sides," Charlotte soothed. "I'm just trying to see things from all angles. What I was going to go on to say, if you'd let me…" She paused, to check I was listening. "What I was going to say was you seemed to enjoy going."

I thought about it and nodded. Charlotte was right. I *did* enjoy going. I liked having a laugh with everyone and being part of the team. I even liked some of the drills. "I do enjoy it, even though I'm not much good."

"Not much good? Come on, Petra – you've only

been playing for a few months; you're bound not to be that good yet. It's taken me three years to get into the show-jumping team."

"I suppose."

"Do you want to know what I think?"

"What?"

"I think you should go to the tournament. If you hate every second, then fair enough, but if you enjoy playing for even one second, despite falling out with Megan, you'll know you should keep going. Otherwise you'll always feel you've let yourself down."

I didn't say anything. I stared at the ground for a few moments, taking in what she had said. Then I looked up and gave her a watery smile. "Don't forget your KitKat," I said, and trudged back to the house.

12

As soon as I stepped into the kitchen, Mum thrust a basket full of wet washing into my arms. "Go and hang these out for me, Petra, there's a good girl."

I took the basket with a heavy sigh. I had wanted to go to my bedroom and think over what Charlotte had said – but I guessed the garden was as good a place as any.

"Oh, Petra, Hannah just called," Mum said as I turned towards the door. "She was wondering why you weren't at practice yesterday, so I told her."

I twisted round. "What did you tell her?"

"I told her you'd lost interest and wouldn't be going any more."

"Oh," I said.

"That *is* what you told me last night?" Mum asked.

"Yes," I mumbled, "it was," and I headed for the garden.

As I hung the washing out, bending down for an item of laundry, then reaching up on tiptoes to peg it on the line, the cement in my stomach started churning and churning. So Hannah knew I had left the team. It was official.

I should have felt relieved, but I didn't. I felt awful – and that's when I knew Charlotte was right. I had given up too easily and I didn't just feel bad about it, I felt terrible.

Leaving the rest of the washing, I dashed inside. Quickly, I searched for the last Parrs newsletter, found Hannah's mobile number and dialled. Luckily she answered straight away. If I'd got her message service, I would have bottled it.

"Hannah?" I asked, my voice all croaky.

"It is. Is that Petra?"

Instead of the word "yes" a sort of strangled sound emerged, a bit like when Dylan does her chicken impression.

"Are you all right?" Hannah asked.

I managed half a grunt.

"Your mum was telling me you don't want to play any more."

"No ... I mean yes ... I mean I didn't but I do now," I said, swallowing hard.

"You do? That's brilliant! It wouldn't be the same without you."

"Really?"

"Really!"

I was a bit surprised by how forcefully Hannah said it. I mean, I don't want to harp on but, as I might have mentioned once or twice, I am not that great a player.

"You know, I'll never forget that Sunday when I first met you and Megan," Hannah continued. "I can see you now, listening so intently as I showed you how to shoot..."

I tried not to but I couldn't help smiling. That was one of my favourite memories too: just me and Megan messing about in the goal.

"And you cracked me up telling me Megan was high-maintenance."

"Oh yeah!"

"But it was you I noticed first, taking those penalties."

"Was it?"

"You were my first Parsnip." She laughed.

I had such a surge of emotion I thought I'd faint. "I was?"

"You were."

Her *first* Parsnip! *First.* I was so used to being second with everyone – second with Mum to Charlotte, second with Charlotte to Betty Boo, second with Megan to Jenny-Jane and football – that hearing I was first to someone was such a shock! And of all the people to be first with, I'd never thought it would be Hannah Preston, our coach and captain of the Parrs. "I didn't know that," I whispered.

"Well, it's true."

"Thank you."

"Look, I know you and Megan have had a bit of a domestic. That's why I phoned earlier."

"Um … you could say that."

"And I'm guessing things are a bit awkward at the moment?"

My voice deserted me again.

"Between you, me and the goalpost, Megan does take her football a bit too seriously at times."

"Tell me about it!"

"But please don't be put off, Petra. Katie and me just want you all to enjoy taking part, whatever your reasons are for coming."

"I know."

"So if you do want to play on Saturday, I can always pick you up."

"Could you?"

"Sure."

I took a deep breath. "OK, then, yes please. I'd love a lift."

"Brilliant!"

I hung up, feeling happier than I had done in days. I was going to the tournament. I was going to play football. It felt … right.

13

On Saturday morning we were tripping over each other, toing and froing, packing this and sorting out that. I was just glad I only had a small kit bag to fill and not a whole horsebox.

When Hannah beeped her horn, I gave Charlotte a tight hug. "Good luck," I told her. "I know you're going to win."

"Don't!" she pleaded. "I'll probably fall off in the first round."

"That's true," I said. "You've polished Betty Boo so much you'll slip right off her!"

She laughed. "I'll text you, whatever happens."

"Back at you."

I then turned to Mum and hugged her, too.

"You're what?" Mum had said when I told her about

changing my mind. "I still can't believe you're going to football instead of show jumping," she said now.

"Believe it, Mum!" I told her and kissed her cheek.

I felt a bit hyper as I hurried to the front gate.

14

In the car, Hannah filled me in on all the details I needed to know. We'd be playing three matches in the first round, all six minutes each way. We had Southfields Athletic first, then the Tembridge Vixens and finally the Misslecott Goldstars.

"Southfields again?"

"Yep."

"Not the Grove Belles, then?" I asked. The Grove Belles were the best team around.

Hannah shook her head. "Not you as well! That's the first thing they asked me at training. Why is everyone so fixated with the Grove Belles?"

"Because it'd be like playing Manchester United or Arsenal Ladies," I said, repeating what I knew from Megan.

"That's what they'd like you to think," Hannah replied. She shook her head. "All Katie and I want from today is for you to have fun. That's what it's about at this level."

We arrived at Ashtonby Sports Club at about half-past nine. It was a huge complex, much bigger than Lornton FC. It was modern, too, with a brightly painted clubhouse that had a swimming pool and a gym besides all the surrounding lush playing fields. "See what I meant about them having the facilities?" Hannah asked.

"Oh yes."

Hannah had arranged to meet everybody by the drinks machine in the main entrance. It was teeming with people. There was such a buzz! Katie was there, as were Tabinda with her parents and Nika with hers. Holly and her dad came next, followed by Amy with her mum. Amy's mum stood out, not only because she had so much make-up on but also because she had this loud voice that carried across everybody's heads. "Oh, isn't this sooo sweet? Don't they all look adorable in their little kits?"

Gemma and Lucy arrived together, and finally Megan and Jenny-Jane. My heart was beating like mad in anticipation. I didn't have a clue how Megan was going to react to seeing me. It had been over a week since we'd fallen out.

Mrs Fawcett waved to me, and my cheeks turned pink as I waved back – but Megan didn't glance my way once. Not once! Jenny-Jane's eyes flicked over me, but she didn't say anything either, she just followed Megan to the far side of the drinks machine, out of my line of vision. I felt wobbly then. So we still weren't talking, and Megan still didn't want to be friends. At that moment, if I could have, I'd have turned round and gone straight home.

"OK, gang? Are we all here?" Hannah asked.

"All except the twins," Holly said in her exasperated way.

"There's time yet. Go and get changed, then meet me out on the field."

15

Before we began, all the teams gathered around a podium in the middle of the playing fields. Two men in tracksuits and a woman in a sun-dress were standing behind a table on which were displayed a gold-coloured trophy and a box full of medals. The woman in the sun-dress said she was a town councillor and the two men were managers of Ashtonby Sports Club. The woman welcomed us and went on about how wonderful it was to see so many girls playing football now and how we were giving the boys a run for their money. "Especially at international level!"

Then she handed the mike over to one of the club managers, who didn't look too impressed by her comments but who said the same thing as Hannah had, that no matter who won this "fabulous trophy"

this afternoon, it was meant to be a fun occasion
– and he pointed out the bouncy castle and ice-
cream van and assorted stalls to prove it. "… So
if the coaches would like to lead their teams to
their allotted pitches, we'll begin this year's Girls'
Summer Football Tournament…"

All the parents and visitors clapped and all the
players cheered. Holly and Nika linked their arms
through mine. It felt so strange not linking with
Megan, but I smiled gratefully at them. I didn't know
if they knew something was wrong between me
and Megan – they didn't say anything – but whether
they did or not it was nice to cross the field with
someone.

We threw our water bottles in a heap by the far
touchline and then followed Hannah as she led us
though our warm-ups. Across from us, Southfields,
in pale blue shirts and deep blue shorts, were doing
the same, but without much enthusiasm. Their
coach was talking to another woman next to her,
not really concentrating. Still, that didn't count for

anything. Hannah had told us not to go in thinking we'd win just because we had the last time. "We were both new then. They've had as much time to improve as we have."

I took up my position at the back, butterflies battering my stomach. I tried not to think about Megan behind me. "You're here now. You might as well have fun and enjoy it!" I ordered myself as the ref blew her whistle.

I'm going to cut to the chase here. Southfields may have had time to improve, but if they had it didn't show. Their headless-chicken impersonations were excellent. We were five–nil up by half-time. I didn't have to do much in defence except watch. To be honest, I was more bothered about having Megan behind me than about having Southfields in front of me. It really freaked me out not being able to turn round and give her a reassuring thumbs-up every time we scored. "Played, girls!" Hannah called as we ran off. "Make sure you have plenty of water."

We only had a minute and then it was time to swap round. Hannah took me, Holly and Eve off and replaced us with Lucy, Jenny-Jane and Amy. I didn't mind – swapping over was what we expected.

It wasn't long before we scored again. Nika scored first, followed by another goal from Gemma and another from Nika. And another. And another. I think even Amy got one.

"I feel sorry for Southfields," I said, seeing how dejected they looked.

"I feel sorry for Megan. She looks fed up," Eve replied.

"She's well bored," Holly said.

"I dunno. I mean, I know she gets nervous but she's quieter than usual. Is something wrong with her, Petra?" Eve asked me.

"No idea." I shrugged, keeping my eyes on the play, where they belonged.

We won eleven–nil in the end. We waited until Southfields had moved out of earshot before whooping and hugging each other.

"Girls, you played really well," Hannah congratulated us.

"Outstanding!" Katie nodded.

Hannah drew us closer. "But this next one will test you. Tembridge are pretty solid. Meggo, you'll need to be on your guard. Full beam ahead."

"I'll try," Megan said in a quiet voice.

I couldn't help but look across at her. Megan never gave timid responses – ever. She had her head down, plucking at the grass, so she didn't see me staring. Jenny-Jane did, though. For once she had her fringe pulled off her face with a hairband and I saw her forehead furrow. I looked away quickly.

16

We had about fifteen minutes' recovery time before the second match started.

Katie took us to one side, and we practised passing and turning with the ball for half the time and mingled with parents the rest of it. I felt a bit left out then. I knew I wasn't the only one without parents there, but it would have been nice to go and stand with Dad or Charlotte or Mum and have a chat. I rummaged in my bag and checked my mobile, in case Charlotte had sent a text, but there was nothing in my inbox. I sent her one instead, telling her our score. HOW BOUT U? I asked. HAV U SLIPPED OFF BB YET? By the time I'd done that, our next team, the Tembridge Vixens, in black and white striped shirts and black shorts, had arrived.

Katie read out the squad names to start. Even

though the twins still hadn't turned up, I wasn't selected.

We had a different referee this time, a stern-faced woman with a nose stud, wearing an Ashtonby FC tracksuit. She blew the whistle and we were off. Match two already!

The Vixens won the toss and kicked off. They were good! No headless chickens in sight.

I noticed how they kept the ball close to their feet and seemed to know where each of their team-mates would be when they passed. The action was in our half mostly and we were soon two–nil down. For the first goal Megan went the wrong way, and for the second, though she blocked the shot with her hands, the ball rebounded straight at a nearby Vixen's foot. Megan'd be really annoyed with herself for the second one, I knew. Not that I was bothered. I just knew she would be, that was all.

At half-time Hannah told everyone not to worry.
"You're doing really well – two goals down against
this team is no disgrace! Just make sure you all
mark up and take every opportunity that comes.
Right…" She looked down at her notepad. "Gemma,
you go on for JJ; Tabs, you go on for Holly; Petra…"
She paused and then glanced across at Megan for
some reason. "Petra, I'm going to try you up front
instead of Eve. OK?"

I shrugged, pretending I hadn't noticed the funny
look. "Sure," I said.

I'd never played up front before. Eve had to point
out where I should stand. "Next to that number 3.
Watch her; she really sticks to you."

"Thanks," I said, and took a deep breath.

We kicked off. The Vixens were quick to mark up
but we managed to keep possession for a while,
especially as Gemma and Tabinda were now in the
middle. Gemma surprised the girl marking her, and
me watching her, by doing this step-over thing with

the ball, and then kind of sliding it across with the outside of her foot to Tabinda. I didn't remember doing those during training!

I felt my heart thumping as I backed closer to the goal in case Tabinda passed to me, but she didn't – or rather, couldn't. She was bundled off the ball before she could do anything. Hannah shouted "Ref!" but the nose-stud lady didn't blow for a foul or anything. Tabinda shrugged, threw her plaits behind her shoulders and ran back towards the action.

The next second I saw the ball fly just over our crossbar and heard the crowd let out a loud "Oooh!" at the near miss. Megan took the goal kick, but she seemed to direct it to nowhere in particular and it went straight out of play near the halfway line. Her nerves must be really bad for her to do that, I thought; either that or she was tired from staying up half the night chatting and giggling with Jenny-Jane. Bet that was it. Bet you anything.

I swallowed hard and focused on the game.

The Vixens' throw-in, quick as anything, found their number 7. She made a run through the middle, but Gemma was there and took the ball off her. It was all so fast it made me dizzy watching.

In what seemed like no time at all, Gemma was tearing towards me and I thought I'd better do something useful, so I ran towards the goal too. Unfortunately, my marker ran with me and blocked me so well that whichever way I dodged, she was there too. I just couldn't escape! But it didn't matter, because Gemma was doing fine on her own. Out of the corner of my eye I saw her take a shot. She was well outside the box, but the ball whizzed straight through a gap in the defence and into the left-hand side of the goal. Yes!

There was no chance of us not celebrating this one. We all dived on Gemma, rubbing her hair, slapping her back and hugging her to pieces, poor thing! "Quality! Quality!" I heard the Vixens coach, a young guy with a shaved head, say. I turned and saw he was clapping Gemma's goal and laughing with Hannah and Katie. I didn't know coaches were so friendly with each other. I thought they were meant to be enemies or something.

"Nice goal," my marker said to me.

"Yeah," I said. "She's our best player."

"She's good."

I felt proud of Gemma then. It didn't matter that she was way better than I'd ever be; it just mattered that I was on the same team. "Yes," I said, "she is."

I wish I could say we equalized straight after, but I can't. In the end it was four–one to them.

"See you then, Parsnip," my marker said at the end.

"You too, Vixen," I replied.

"Brilliant, brilliant, brilliant!" Hannah gushed as we gathered round our pile of stuff.

"Er ... we lost!" Lucy reminded her.

"Course you did! They were second in the league last season. What do you expect?"

"Second! No wonder they were so good!" Tabinda moaned.

"Exactly! They've been in the league for two seasons and we haven't even started yet. You guys were fantastic!" Katie told us. "You just kept right at 'em." Her eyes were shining. "I think we've got the makings of something here, don't you, Miss Preston?"

Hannah nodded. "I do, Miss Regan, I do."

17

For the third match we had to move pitches.

"Right," Hannah said after we'd dumped our stuff in a pile on the edge of the new touchline and had a drink. "What I've noticed is you're not challenging enough. You're reluctant to get tackles in at the right time – but you've got to make that ball *yours* … so let's do some work on that. Into fours quickly…"

For someone who'd told me we were meant to be having fun, Hannah was taking each match very seriously, I thought as I hurriedly attached myself to Lucy, Tabinda and Eve in case I somehow ended up with Megan. Luckily Megan and JJ didn't join in with us, so I needn't have panicked. Katie took them across to one of the goals, further away from us. I didn't know what they were doing. It was none of my business.

☆ ☆ ☆

I didn't play at all against the Misslecott Goldstars.
I was a bit surprised not to be put on in the second
half (we were two-all), but I didn't mind too much.
Apart from Megan in goal, Hannah was swapping
and changing us round all the time. Maybe I'd been
on more than some of the others, I didn't know.
I just concentrated on the game.

The Goldstars weren't totally inexperienced like
Southfields and they weren't dead good like the
Vixens. The ball went up and down and off and on
the pitch like a wasp stuck in a jar, with most of the
action in the middle. Final score? We drew three-all.
I can't tell you what their goals were like, because
I wasn't looking *that* end. Ours were from a corner
taken by Nika and scored by Gemma, and two from
the box tapped in by Eve.

"What happens now?" I asked Lucy when the
final whistle blew.

"I don't know," she said. "We need to check out
the table."

☆ ☆ ☆

The table, a huge whiteboard on wheels parked near the podium, had all the match results mapped out.

The results for our group looked like this:

GROUP 1

GAME 1

Parrs U11s 11   Southfields Athletic U11s 0
Misslecott Goldstars 2   Tembridge Vixens 6

GAME 2

Parrs U11s 1   Tembridge Vixens 4
Southfields Athletic U11s 2   Misslecott Goldstars 9

Game 3

Misslecott Goldstars 3   Parrs U11s 3
Tembridge Vixens 14   Southfields Athletic U11s 0

We all silently scrutinized the results for a few moments, taking in all the information.

I concentrated on the table. It was still in alphabetical order rather than points order.

Team	P	F	A	W	D	L	Pts
Misslecott Goldstars	3	14	11	1	1	1	4
Parrs Utts	3	15	7	1	1	1	4
Southfields Athletic	3	2	34	0	0	3	0
Tembridge Vixens	3	24	3	3	0	0	9

The Vixens had won every match so they automatically went through, but Misslecott Goldstars and us were on the same points. "It's down to goal difference," I heard Megan say, her voice trembling.

"Yep," Hannah said, patting her shoulder, "good old goal difference."

"We've got five more than them," I pointed out before anyone else did. I'm in maths club – I'm quick at spotting these things. "We go through!"

Everyone cheered except Megan, who gave me a sideways glance but didn't say anything. As everyone chatted, I cleared my throat a few times and focused on my boots, trying to pretend it didn't bother me. If this was how it was going to be from now on, then I'd better get used to it.

Katie began telling us what a real achievement it was that we'd made it to the semifinals: "Especially considering how new we are and how widespread our age range is!"

"Who're we playing next?" Lucy asked.

"Looks like you all got your wish!" Hannah said, tapping the adjoining sheet of results.

"Not the Grove Belles?" Eve gasped.

"Oh yeah! Who else?"

The Grove Belles. Manchester United and Arsenal Ladies in one. The team who'd been top of the Nettie Honeyball League every year since it began (2001). The team who'd won the Nettie Honeyball Cup every year since the Nettie Honeyball Cup began (2002). *Those* Grove Belles.

"Cool," said Lucy.

18

We had three-quarters of an hour's break this time. The tension was mounting; you could feel it in the warm summer air. We did a few drills, but mainly we were allowed to wander around, go to the loo, have a snack and relax. Amy chose to sunbathe on the blanket her mum had brought.

Of course normally I'd have been with Megan, but now that wasn't an option, so instead I kind of hovered on the edge of different groups. Once again I noticed that Megan and Jenny-Jane went off by themselves. So chummy. The heavy-pastry feeling kept coming back but I tried to ignore it by asking everybody loads of questions. I found out that Holly was going on holiday to Florida straight after the tournament, and that both of Eve's brothers were at Leicester City's summer school this week, and that Lucy's brother had been grounded – but she didn't say why.

All too soon it was time for the semifinal. The crowd had grown – the lady in the sun-dress came to watch, along with a few other parents and girls in their kits from teams I didn't recognize but supposed had been knocked out.

"I don't like it," Holly said to me, "so many people watching."

"I do!" Amy beamed. "It's good practice for when I'm on the catwalk."

I wasn't sure how I felt. I definitely had butterflies in my stomach now instead of pastry, but they weren't doing crazy somersaults or anything. I felt – I don't know – *apart* from it all … as if I was there but not there.

Hannah and Katie gathered us round for a group huddle. We waited for Hannah's words of wisdom. "Just go out there and be awesome," she said.

We all looked at her. Was that it?

As if she'd read our minds, Katie said, "Just do your best."

The scrum dissolved and we were told our positions. Again, I was a sub. Unfortunately, so was Jenny-Jane. I stood as far away from her as I could, but for every sideways step I took, she took one too, though neither of us spoke. She was probably as awestruck as I was when the Grove Belles took their positions.

I could tell straight away that the Belles were in a different league from the other teams we'd played. The way they walked onto the pitch and took up their positions without fuss, as if they'd done it a thousand times before. The way they seemed to radiate light from their all-white (and still super-clean) kit. The way they began by either jumping up and down on the spot or twisting their hips from side to side, as if raring to go. The way they shouted out to each other: "Play up, Belles!" and "On your toes, people!" It was intimidating.

They were also huge. Massive. Either tall and

lanky or tall and stocky. Under 11s? No way! If I'd been speaking to Jenny-Jane, I'd have said something like, "If that's their Under 11s team, what's their Under 12s like? *Shrek?*" If I'd been speaking to her. Which I wasn't, so I didn't.

The stern-faced referee we'd had for the Vixens game had a brief word with Hannah, then went to stand on the touchline opposite. She must be their coach, I realized. She didn't look half as friendly as the Vixens one. And not a hundredth as friendly as Hannah and Katie.

Our referee this time was one of the tracksuited blokes from the podium. He blew the whistle and we were off. "Come on, Parsnips! You can do this!" the parents on our side cheered.

The Belles won the toss and kicked off. They had the ball in our box – and their first goal – within four passes. That fast – one-two-three-four and in! Ouch! They caught us napping – especially Megan. Any other day she would have saved the shot, as it didn't have that much power behind it, but it bounced out of her arms and over her shoulder.

"That's your fault," JJ hissed, as the Belles celebrated.

"Mine?" I said, giving her a look.

"She's totally off her game because of you. She can't concentrate at all."

No way was she getting away with that. No way did I have to creep round Jenny-Jane Bayliss today. "Huh! For your information, it's *your* fault we're not speaking, not mine."

Jenny-Jane sniffed. "What? 'Cos of the sleepover thing? Pathetic!"

"It might be pathetic to you."

"I thought Hannah was supposed to be having a word? To sort all that out?"

I frowned, not realizing at first what she meant.

"She said she'd phone you," Jenny-Jane prompted.

"She did phone. How did you know?"

"It was me who told her to. Fat lot of good it's done."

I didn't reply, partly because the Belles had

scored again and partly to let what Jenny-Jane had said sink in.

"And as for that whole sleepover thing, I told Megan she was being daft, saying you couldn't be there."

I didn't see that one coming! "Did you?"

"Course. Just 'cos you and me don't see eye to eye doesn't mean we'd show it at her house, does it? Or on the pitch."

I gawped at Jenny-Jane in disbelief. "That's what I told Megan!"

Jenny-Jane shrugged. "I didn't even want to stay at her house; I knew our Bi– … I knew the reason I didn't want to be at home would be out."

"Your brothers?" I said. I kept my voice down so no one could overhear.

She looked at me, as if sussing out how much I knew, then nodded. "Yeah. I knew those two wallies would be in the pub all night celebratin' so they wouldn't be around to get at me."

"Seriously?"

"Seriously. It was inconvenient staying at Megan's, to be honest. I was meant to be babysitting."

"Oh."

"Don't tell her that, though."

"I won't."

"And I didn't sleep a wink. I like my own bed, me."

"Oh."

"Don't tell her that, neither."

"I won't." I blinked, reeling from all this information. It was just so different to what I'd thought had happened.

"And all she did all night was talk about you and what a special friend you are and how upset she was because you'd fallen out and she didn't know what to do. Talk about pass the sick bucket! Like I said to her, what's the big deal? I fall out with my mates all the time."

I frowned. "Well, *we* don't! It's new to us."

"Huh! I worked that one out. Weirdos! You both want to get a life!"

I opened my mouth and closed it again. I just

didn't know what to say – but as Jenny-Jane was still lecturing me it didn't matter.

"You could at least help with her nerves. I've been trying all morning, but nothing works. We're getting hammered out there and we don't need to be."

As if to prove her point, the Belles scored again. "They *are* the best team around," I pointed out.

"They're not all that!" Jenny-Jane said with contempt. "We're giving them too much respect. They just need rattlin', that's all."

We were distracted by more cheers from the crowd opposite. The Belles had scored *again*. What was that – four or five? To rub it in, the Grove players didn't even celebrate. They had bored expressions on their faces, as if they couldn't be bothered.

Megan picked the ball out of the back of the net. She looked as dejected as the whole of Southfields Athletic put together. "If you were any sort of mate you'd do something, Wardy. And quick," Jenny-Jane told me. "Even Hannah can't sort this one." She walked away, leaving me with my head spinning.

19

At half-time Hannah gave everyone a hug.
"Come on, girls, heads up, now. We've done well to get this far."

No one agreed. It wasn't because we were losing – we'd expected that – it was because we knew we could do so much better, like Jenny-Jane had said. For the first time I realized how Megan and me falling out had affected the whole team. Gemma might be the best player, but Megan was the leader, the one who yelled encouragement and fired everyone up. She hadn't done that today because she'd been upset. I admit I felt a tiny, tiny bit chuffed then – it took something huge to distract Megan from her football, and for her, like for me, falling out was huge. But we hadn't fallen out any more. She just didn't know it yet.

Hannah checked her notebook. "OK, let's have Nika off for JJ and Tabs off for Amy. Er..." She looked at Megan. "Meggo, do you want a break?"

Megan scowled and her eyes filled with tears. "No!"

"You sure?"

"Definitely!"

I was amazed Hannah had even asked such a dumb question. This was Megan Phoebe Fawcett she was talking to! In it to the bitter end.

Hannah gave her another lingering look, then checked her notes. "OK. Petra on for..."

You know I said the butterflies in my stomach weren't going crazy or anything? Cut that. They'd woken up big-time and decided to throw a party. Even the heavy-pastry feeling would have been preferable to the whirlpool my tummy had become. I took a deep breath. "Please may I go in defence?" I asked, in case she put me in Eve's position again.

Hannah looked at me searchingly. "You sure?"

"Definitely."

"OK, then, you swap with ... Holly."

I nodded and gave Holly a high five.

"Good luck. They're so fast," Holly told me.

I followed Megan onto the pitch as we took up our positions for the second half. I knew she was nervous and upset. I couldn't do much about the nerves, but I could stop her from being upset, like Jenny-Jane had for me. I had to let her know I wanted to be friends again, and I did it in the only way I knew how. "Lor, Miss Fawcett, you'll forgive me for saying so, but I can't 'elp but notice your on-field performance has been lackin' a bit," I told her in my best Dickens.

Megan turned, giving me a fierce scowl. "Don't you…" she began – then stopped because she could see that I was smiling. Her eyes shone and her shoulders sagged with relief. "Well, Miss Ward, that may well be true. I fear I have been rather distracted of late," she said with a dramatic sniff.

As for me, I just wanted to cry, but that would have done no good at all. Instead I returned to my normal voice and let her have it. "Distracted? What kind of lame excuse is that, you big wimp? Ha! Watch and learn, Fawcett," I said. "I'm going to get Man of the Match after this half ... or whatever you get on a girls' team."

She snorted and tapped her red bandana for luck. It was the first time I'd seen her do that all tournament. It meant she was back! "In your dreams, Wardy."

"In your sweaty armpits, Fawcett."

"In your greasy earwax."

"In your crusty bogies."

"Shut up."

"You shut up."

"High five?"

"High ten!"

As we smacked hands, we heard a round of applause from the touchline. Turning, we saw Hannah and Katie clapping us. How embarrassing!

"What's that about?" Megan asked.

"Don't ask me," I told her.

20

The Belles thought they had us licked.

They walked back on with such a casual air about them. Big mistake. We'd been told to be awesome, so we were. As soon as the whistle blew, Gemma and JJ blazed in the middle, fighting for every ball. I could see what Jenny-Jane had meant about rattling them. *She* was like a wasp now, not in a jar this time but in a pair of baggy knickers! The Belles tried to swat her away – and only made her more irritated when they did. The trouble was, once she had the ball she wouldn't let it go to anyone else, on either side. She'd run with it for a bit, then have a wild shot from anywhere, but too often it went out for a goal kick or a throw-in. Still, the Belles didn't like the change of pace. They were shouting more to each other and their coach was bellowing instructions from the touchline. "Who's on number 8?" and "That's yours, Becky!" and "One of you!"

For my part, I was sticking with their number 23, a short-haired girl with a long nose. She used her long nose to look down at me, reminding me instantly of a horse. That was a pity. For her.

Then the ball was with the Belles again and coming this way. I thought my heart would stop! Their centre crossed to the left wing and found their number 7. I sensed Horseface was about to make a run from our wing into the box, but I kept with her, darting in front with my back to her, and we ended up doing this sort of weird dance together near the dead-ball line. She muttered something under her breath, then I felt her shove me hard in the back. The whistle blew and I thought it was because of that – but it wasn't.

The referee was running to the other side, where the Belles' number 7 was rolling about on the ground, clutching her ankle. Above her, Jenny-Jane was shrugging Lucy away as she tried to restrain her and yelling at the Grove player to get up. "You're not on telly, you know, you dirty diving diva..." and then she let out a string of swear words I can't repeat or I'd be grounded for life.

The referee blew for a direct free kick to them – and as soon as he did, the number 7 was on her feet and running to take it.

Unfortunately that annoyed Jenny-Jane even more. "That's how you win all the time, is it? By cheating? Falling over fresh air?" she called out, chasing after her.

"Referee! That's harassment!" their coach called out from the side.

The referee nodded and called Jenny-Jane over to have a word.

"Uh-oh," said Megan.

"What?"

"She's not very good with authority figures."

I could tell. Jenny-Jane was arguing away and in the end the referee called for Hannah to take her off, though he did allow Holly to replace her.

"Good rattling," I told Jenny-Jane as she stormed past.

She looked at me and grinned.

21

We'd never done a free kick before in a match and had only practised them a couple of times. There were four of us in the wall: me, Holly, Gemma and Lucy. Behind us, Megan called out instructions. "Left a bit – I can't see," she shouted. "No, not that much!"

We shuffled along until Megan was happy and the ref was happy and the number 7 was happy. "Bend it like Becky, Becky!" the Belles coach called out, and everyone in the Belles crowd laughed.

"Hold steady!" Hannah called to us.

I was shaking. My heart was pumping. The butterflies in my stomach were doing the samba, and for the first time, as I waited for this girl I'd never met in my life to try to score against my team – *my* team with *me* in it – I got it. I really, really got it.

What playing football was all about. Ten out of ten.

Becky placed the ball and stepped back five, six, seven paces. There was a hush as she ran and kicked. *Whack!* I twisted round as the ball flew past us and watched as Megan leapt majestically and palmed it away for a corner. *Yes!* We ran to mob her, celebrating as if we'd won the tournament. "Brilliant!" "Great save!" "Go Meggo!"

"Gerroff me!" Megan protested – but I could see she was chuffed.

The Belles had already lined up to take the corner. Again, I marked up Horseface and prevented her from getting anything out of it. Lucy saved the day this time, by heading the cross out of danger and onto the unmarked Gemma.

For once, the Belles were caught off guard. Everyone had been crowding round our goal, so there was no one in midfield to stop Gemma and no one back in defence apart from the goalie. It was one on one. "Go on, Gemma! Go on!" we all screamed. Their goalie came off her line and dived dramatically at Gemma's feet, but Gemma checked herself in time, sidestepped the goalie and tapped the ball into the net, calm as you like. We had scored! We had scored against the Belles!

And the crowd went wild! Even the lady in the sun-dress was jumping up and down. I thought my lungs would explode, I whooped so much.

The ref had to blow his whistle about six times before we were brought to order. Mintiness overload!

I'd like to say we made a dramatic comeback after that, but come on – keep it real. The Belles made two substitutions, turned it up a notch and scored twice more before the end of the match. We'd lost seven–one – but it didn't matter. We walked off with our heads held high. Megan and me had our arms round each other's shoulders like we always do and then I called Jenny-Jane across to join us. The three amigos!

22

Katie and Hannah called us together for a post-match hug and made us all big-headed by telling us how fantastic we'd been. "That was brilliant! True teamwork," Hannah beamed before going through our good points individually. "... and as for Petra ... what ace man-marking! You'll be fantastic at jockeying when we look at that."

"Jockeying? No thanks! I don't want anything to do with horses!" I laughed – then my mouth flew open. "Horses! Hang on, guys! Back in a tick!" I untangled myself and dashed to my bag and found my mobile.

There was a text from Charlotte. About time! Her team had come sixth out of thirty-two; that's pretty impressive. She had told me they'd be ecstatic to reach the top ten. DIDN'T SLIP OFF BB ONCE! RESULT!! she put.

I sent her a quick text back congratulating her and telling her about our team. I had just pressed SEND when I felt a tug on my elbow. I turned to see Daisy McNeil, in full kit, staring at me. Behind her were the rest of her family – Dylan, her mum and dad, and her twin brothers, Declan and Darwin.

"Hello, Petrasaurus," Daisy said, "have we missed anything?"

"No, Daisy," I told her, trying not to laugh. "Not a single thing!"